SO-FAE-456

RADIO PICASSO

RADIO PICASSO

POEMS AND DRAWINGS

Steve McCabe

watershedBooks

Copyright © text and drawings Steve McCabe 1999
All rights reserved

No part of this book may be reproduced, stored in a retrieval system, or transmitted in any form, by any means, electronic or mechanical, without permission in writing from the publisher, except by a reviewer who may quote brief passages in a review.

"Coal", "Oregon Trail Shoulders", "The Knuckles of a Killer", and "The Prehistoric Films of India" were previously published in *Understatement: An Anthology of Twelve Poets* (Seraphim Editions, 1996). "Magritte and Me" was previously published in *ars poetica* (Art Bar/Letters Workshop, 1996).

A.F. Moritz, Editor
Cover art: Steve McCabe
Book and cover design by Bernard Kelly, Perkolator {Kommunikation}.
Author's photo by T. Nanavati.

Typeset in Perpetua.
Printed in Canada by The Coach House Printing Co., Toronto.

watershedBooks
71 Fermanagh Ave.
Toronto, Ontario, Canada M6R 1M1

Canadian Cataloguing in Publication Data

McCabe, Steve, 1949-
          Radio Picasso
Poems.
ISBN 1-894205-03-0
I. Title.
PS8575.C2925R32 1999   C811'.54   C99-930879-3
PR9199.3M34R32 1999

For Tannaz

Contents

Radio Picasso

Through a radio to a torso   beyond
A small city heavy with labor   breeding
                                    its own smallness.

I leaned out a storm window into history
So vivid,
        the paint was still drying,

And I rubbed its stomach.

Radio Picasso update: (Afro-cubist);   sweeping blonde –
Marie Thérèse,
News and weather   buried
Beneath rough hued brush static.

Men covered in sawdust   silently
                                   chewed.

Their lunchboxes   aluminum.
Their eyes shuttered.
Weeds growing through   cracked
Concrete. Broken bits of   coral
                                 a reminder;

Blue Mediterranean/baby Paulo/diagonal mask;
White fear of Matisse.

A matador's blade
Pulled up and out. Peggy Guggenheim cooing
Over a dismantled handlebar
(On the A.M. band),   turn it off.

Radio Picasso illegal in the motherland.

Pull down the black shade.

Those ol' boys at the barbershop unsure
        of the exact location
        of the frequency they   avoid

                fought a war against   book burners
And never opened one   again.

A shaved face is like a blank piece of paper —
There's no need to listen.

In the house with cracked walls,
My mother painted by number,
And my father thinned his blood with bourbon.

Radio Picasso   was a river and the good citizens
Built dams   he couldn't swim just splashed
For the camera,
His eye   was a lens,
Never   needing civic council approval,
Squeezing   energy out of every orifice.

The minotaur and satyr kick inside his fleshy heels
                doing up the town.

In the shadow of Guernica, he mixes   black and white,
                                          at night
The distant stations come in   clearer.
Two mistresses fistfight
                for his power —
Tilted faces/frenzied and furious/writhing horses/dying.
Did he identify with the terror or explosions
                        or the blueness
Or the International Brigade?

Twist the dial. Fold a white napkin.

Haphazardous planks crisscrossing
Resemble bombers skimming
Grapevines, burning skin
With putrid glee.

An odor of pulp from the mill   upstream
Swings like a lantern in the frozen   air
Above the killer whale DeSoto
(With its little, *almost,* fins)
Still cold
          After idling half an hour.

Wedged   in
Shoulder to shoulder, our breath   escaping
Us like the   steam
Above the porridge Mother cooked
          with raisins.

Dora Maar pours him another glass of   razorblade
                                       sugar.
Could he destroy her   too?

Her leopardskin King on a triangular chessboard.
Paris in the 20's: a rose to cut your face
When you starve
          and he doesn't.

Keep the volume inside your head listening
          to Radio Picasso.

Sparrow beaks scissor crystals.
Our skin wished it was rabbit fur.
Our eyeballs were shaved heads feeling the wonder
Of the morning prison.

Each night the cold burned
To keep knowledge out of our bodies.

A cubist still life: Georges Braque's epitome of
        perfection;
                left in the dust –
                        sound effects
                with a sidecar/kickstarting the next
Phase: Picasso invented reinventing –
        he didn't need to include himself.

Listen to the sunlight in his room
                        in the early morning,
The radio like a castle.

Jacqueline opens a window   to erase
The smell of   death.
Life magazine comes calling. You know the   frequency
By heart.

Advertising is history, whispering   full blast
Beneath your pillow, when you're supposed to be asleep.

Faraway places seem possible.
Overseas transmissions newscast his staggering talent.
A portion seems possible.

The blue and white striped shirts in Dufy's sailboats
                don't rip up history:
Radio Picasso is a carnivore. His tail the antenna.

His women are the bull in the bullfight.
His red cape cloaks other signals.

My mother fills the sink to wash more dishes.

The disoriented river, a stone's throw away,

Blinded by bleach and chlorine,
Rises against the hand of ice
Embroidered from its own skin.

My father eased the car into the slipstream:
A numb procession of switchblades
Eager for teeth and victory.

My gloved finger crudely creates portholes
To observe a world misting over.

Radio Picasso has sex   frequently,
Sleeps and   urinates,
Discards beautiful   angels
Bent beyond recognition.
They are his national anthem.

Salute his meat cleaver eyebrows, going in
              for the kill,
                        "I will paint you."

Spanish sorrow with bent fingers
              scratching the inside of the cabinet.

Waves of exuberant   flesh
Passing outside the studio window,

Radio Picasso broadcasting   bone.

You to You

My hand covers the rise of your flesh
Containing – how should I say it –
The sun within the moon.

As if weary fish eager for evolution
Happened upon rooms of dry land
Behind watery doors.

My body heat performs the ritual of alchemy
Or perhaps dowsing is a better word –
Conducting you to you.

I am an abstract ellipse
One aspect of the curve you are travelling
To yourself.

I orbit you and you stick to me
Like gravity drowning what's inside your chest
Unseen doors open and close.

The secrecy that nature is hinged on
Electrifies my hand
With the memory of your memories.

Lava

Within temple walls and my prescribed boundaries
An elixir etches my hope with opposites

You think the thoughts thought by others
Your beauty is defined by cracked marble

A moon laced with rivers of lava
Alights in a meadow populated by spiky horrors

Should I be told the truth
Or is the lava in my eye?

And are you shining full and golden
Above a perfect temple?

Tiger Iris

My children remember/my moustache and eyebrows
Turning into a dead man's

                                               ghost/
The day the   sun
Broke I lifted them into another   dimension.

When I woke my arms and legs fell asleep
Next to a cold window she pulls on her socks
Laughing, sinking her roots into my chest
Pulling me out of exile/whispering my

                                               name.

Her spine is like a snake at the fishgate
Reviving me with soft grinding/

                        teeth on my neck
                        blood on my cheekbone
Her tiger iris is curved into her shoulder:
She asks and I answer —

Staring at the vacuum cleaner's shadow
Lifting the lid on my father's coffin.

On the Occasion of
First Meeting My Son

Bleeding doesn't erase my palm
When I break the green spikes open.

You're an egg in my blood
I grow skin to protect you.

You've always been inside me
Where I know myself.

What you need to say has many rooms.

I live inside my voice
Where you should have been.

A light from your window
Is spilling over the edge
Into a space I saved for you.

Transfiguration

A butterfly wing

Grazes your cheek

Travelling

Two thousand years

Per second.

Magritte and Me

René Magritte scoops me off a ledge of sky
His construct of time the white of an eye.

I declare the final vision ...

Okay – so I was twenty-one –
Clarity arrives the proximity of sonar.

Me thinking Magritte a sentinel
For precisely shattered revolution
Him walking on eggshells
A ritual of underwater glass.

The green apple touches four walls
The air a crackling fossil.

Freeze frame ransackers scrape Magritte's feet
Clean – the brilliance of a capitalist heist –
World without end – download the syringe –

Okay – so I'm not twenty-one –
Angular or panicky / walking in milk
Perfectly still
Magritte the great hunter
Taught me how.

"Mark My Grave with a Big, Red, Flashing Neon Arrow" – Roy Lichtenstein

THE NEW YORK TIMES OBITUARIES,
TUESDAY, SEPTEMBER 30, 1997
A PASTICHE

Roy Lichtenstein, the quintessential master of pop painting
And a major figure in American art since he began scavenging
Comics like *Winnie Wilkie, G.I. Combat* and *Secret Hearts*
("I don't care! I'd rather sink – than call Brad for help!"),
Died yesterday at New York University Medical Center
            in Manhattan.
He was 73 and lived in Manhattan.

The cause was complications from pneumonia, said his
            wife, Dorothy.

He apparently died of natural causes, said Dr. Nancy Simmons,
Acting chairwoman of the museum's mammalogy department.

"He was one of the few people of whom it can be truly said
That he was an authority on every kind of bat, all over
            the world."

Mr. Lichtenstein gained attention at his debut in 1962
At the Leo Castelli Gallery in Manhattan with work
That seemed bent on deflating Abstract Expressionism,
With its soul searching claims and its emphasis
On the eloquence of the artist's touch.

In addition, at the American Museum of Natural History
And at other museums, he analyzed specimens
Of different kinds of bats, some of them obtained
100 years ago or more.

By contrast, Mr. Lichtenstein's art looked wicked,
Ironic and freeze dried, as if manufactured, because it
Mimicked in cunningly streamlined form the black outlines,
Flat vivid colors and Ben Day dots of the funny pages.

Perhaps the best known dispute he oversaw
Was the 1965 drive by New York taxicab drivers for a union.
The labor leader Harry Van Arsdale Jr. accused the
        Federal Board
Of failing to address the drivers' grievances.

And if in later years he was sometimes taken for granted,
It was partly because his ideas had so infiltrated art
That they were no longer only his. Mixing text and image,
High and low, his whole strategy of appropriation paved
        the way
For a generation of artists not yet born.

"I can't say I immediately fell in love with the viola,"
He said in a 1977 interview with *The New York Times*.
"I began to play it because in Europe a violin student
Has to play viola as a second instrument."

The dispute dragged on for months until a garage by garage
Election could be conducted.

As a consequence, his own art, he said, was
"Anti-contemplative, anti-nuance, anti-getting-
Away-from-the-tyranny-of-the-rectangle,
Anti-movement and anti-light, anti-mystery,
Anti-paint quality, anti-Zen, and anti-all of those
Brilliant ideas of preceding movements which everyone
        understands
So thoroughly."

A citywide strike by cab drivers was averted.

He also gave violin recitals in Boston in the early 1940's.

Still, it was never easy to know just how seriously to
Take Mr. Lichtenstein. Years later he also said, "I wouldn't
Believe anything I tell you." And it quickly became clear,
After his Castelli debut, that his interests extended beyond
Just making the culture of Mickey Mouse and Bazooka
        Bubble Gum
Wrappers into a new parodic and heraldic art.

He was best known among his peers for his book
Anticipations, Uncertainty and Dynamic Planning, which was
Published in 1940. "This was early and very exciting work ..."

"... Really seminal papers critical to understanding the
Bats of Peru – and the bats of the Sudan."

By the end of the 60's, in fact, he quit using comic book
Sources. Working in one basic mode for the better part of
40 years, he turned out paintings that mimicked Picasso,
Cezanne and Mondrian, treating them in much the same way
That Andy Warhol treated Marilyn Monroe and Elvis Presley:
As brand names of popular culture.

He made his first violin when he was 15 and moved to
Paris four years later to continue his studies.

So, on what had seemed a one liner of an idea,
Mr. Lichtenstein composed unforeseen variations.
They tumbled out like circus clowns from a Volkswagen.

During the 1960's, he served as a consultant
On public finance to the Governments of Chile and Venezuela,
As well as to the Organization of American States.

He also received the Gerrit S. Miller Jr. Award
From the North American Symposium on Bat Research.

To all of these images there was, nonetheless, a particular
And unmistakably American quality: A lean, laconic
Scrutiny of the world that separated his art even from
The paintings of Europeans of his generation, like Richard
Hamilton and Sigmar Polke, who also borrowed from
Pop culture sources.

After a leave for Army service during World War II,
He was assigned to deal with early disputes
After the state introduced rent control in 1946.

On all this and more, however, Mr. Lichtenstein
Said little and revealed less. A trim, slight, shy man
Who in his later years wore his silver hair in a
Tight pony tail, he had a Cheshire cat grin and a
Combination of mocking and self-mocking humor
That masked his seriousness.
"I don't have any big anxieties," he once said.
"I wish I did. I'd be much more interesting."

For a few years he kept himself employed doing
Window displays at Halle's Department Store and
Sheet metal designs for Republic Steel.

By then he was in demand as a freelance chamber player,
And was a frequent guest of the Budapest String Quartet,
The Guarneri Quartet and the Julliard Quartet.
As a soloist he recorded Berlioz's ...

Handbook of Zoology.

In 1958 he appeared as a contestant on the television
Quiz show "Tic Tac Dough." He did so well, winning $42,000,

That he was able to enroll at Columbia University and earned
Undergraduate and master's degrees in history. In 1967, he
        published
The Fall of Japan, an account of the end of the Pacific War.

In the late 60's, when he began to parody Abstract
Expressionist paintings by making works of flat, anonymous
And cartoon-like brush strokes that were the antithesis
Of the brush stroke as a kind of expressive fingerprint
He explained the works by saying:

"I did those pictures because it was my way of
Saying, 'You see, painting is a tree made out of brush strokes.'"

By 1964, *Life* magazine published an article about him
Asking, "Is he the worst artist in America?"

An authority on bats is dead.

"I don't really know what to make of it.
There's something terribly brittle about it. I suppose
I would still prefer to sit under a tree with a picnic basket
Than under a gas pump, but signs and comic strips
Are interesting as subject matter."

Fossil

Fish in a coma
Slept through the ice age waking
Beneath clear water.

Oa

Soothsay (somesay) Mount Oberlin (mount O)
Is / (a) picturesque peak viewed:
Best from / viewed from / Going to the Sun Highway –
Crossing the Continental Divide ÷ by way of Logan's Pass.

Ancient oracles (Oa) traced the highway (not yet created)
                        on maps not yet created
With fingers detonating dynamite   (as if by magic)
Clearing rock / timber / soil along the line
Of their blood a blood   line.

Purity of which (somesay) soothsaying determines how –
A nation's oracles / construct avenues of

                     transport /
A true oracle (Oa) gives his / her life
For / the progress / of the bloodline (not yet created).

False oracles (oFF) with mangled / index / fingers build
Roads which / while appearing normal / natural to the naked
Eye

Under scrutiny are (revealed) passageways to interior
Fault lines / of the earth (or) correspondingly
Bodily organs / destined to premature
Failure.

The beautiful (somesay) Logan's Pass has never / been
Known to have been

                Transversed / by the dead
Or the idea (soothsaying) of   death.

Wagon trains/of the dead/have appeared
Beneath (high)powered micrOscOpes – in the bodies
Of those/deceived/by false oracles.

Fingers return/to original glory
If a (soothsaying) bloodlines accuracy
Has been proven by (somesaying) historical veracity.

The revelations/of Mt. Oberlin/below the earth
In the bodies/of the infected/bear this (truism)
To be true.

Somesay.

A/round

An eye is the same/
Shape as/a star or
Planet/two eyes crossed
Out of focus become one headache/is it
Any wonder we seek/
A mate beyond the core of the earth/
A moon to the sun/symmetry
Of otherness inside looking out/
For/
Number one curving spatially into/
Zero/the sum total
Of two becoming/one heart with valves
Vessels/arteries/underground wells
Flooding yesterday's birth photographed/by
The Hubble telescope/a lens modelled/
After our eye/the same
As a planet rolling in its groove/
Invisibly etched atomic patterns/
Love one another/As I have
Loved you/your pupil a black hole through which
The universe pours/zeroes and
Circumference/round and round we go/where
We stop/no two eyes are the same.

Oregon Trail Shoulders

She soaps the soles of my feet.
I lift one knee like a stag.
She massages my ankle, shin, calf.
Tells me to put my foot down.
Repeats the process.

Her fingers move into my face,
Erasing shadows with white foam.
The near boiling water on my neck
Relaxes my Oregon Trail shoulders.
Eddies of current cross my thighs.
She takes me in her mouth.
We trade places.

I part her jet black hair with loosened fingers.
She is beneath a volcanic waterfall.
I wipe soap off her forehead and nose.

In my other life, wagons roll past fields of tall grass.
In the dry season, lightning storms set this swaying ocean
On fire.
She is lightning and the rain that follows.
Cooking me potatoes with coriander and green onion.

War Smock

Not wrapping the war smock around my head
A thick acrid smoke from a campfire
Ready to rain —

Not deliberating in a war room over the fate
Of your terrain mapping you year by year
Obscuring rainbows
                    or wrapping them
In leg irons my neck hardly able to keep my head upright
Your border eyes reflecting umbrellas.

                    I'm not searching for green salad
With searchlights peeling smoke off my head —
            this smock
Is meant to be worn by a butcher, a painter or
                    a renegade pain collector
        lovers never
                    wear such things as this.

Red Abstraction

Bittersweet angel,
Decreed to exist barely visible; a geometric conceit;
Selecting the finest sugared fruits
From a long lost tree
Invisibly subdivided by years.

The motion of his hands picking and choosing;
He knows what to look for,
The moment of readiness is long living,
Even when he peeks around the corner,
A whirligig reminder:
How red abstraction becomes,
When the abstract has been lost
For a reason too bitter to taste.

The measuring and positioning of the vortex in season,
Striking some of us down like a red flame –
How else can an invasion succeed?

Only bittersweet roots can lay the groundwork
For make believe branches
And a rope swing, blowing in the wind,
Waiting for its passenger beneath the tree
Fruitlessly heavy, with an eternity of weightlessness,
Snapping the rope.

Invisibility subdivided by years
Is how red abstraction becomes;
Waiting to push a child on a swing.
Waiting for laughter over his shoulder.

An invisible offering of sugared fruit
From the tree that is and is not;
The angel that is an undoing principle
Remaining fixed.
While gardens relentlessly Edenic
Appear only to disappear
Beneath the weight of years.

Photographs of invading red flames
Exist as a portrait of love
Proportionate to losses given,
Erupting in season,
Invisibly three dimensional,
A sketchy outline in white
Around sugared fruits in the long lost tree
Growing old in its shadow.

What was has become what is,
Becoming what shall be:
A trinity cycle of angelic calculation
Whispering and unsticking –
The shattering sound dividing
What has ceased from what ceases to be.

The bittersweet arrives with passing years.
Emotions neither too harsh nor too sweet
Finally swinging on a wooden seat.

Beneath the branch,
Pushed by an invisible hand.

The Prehistoric Films of India

They knew how to create
a box of fire
while inside
hands of ash clapped in paradise.

Cultural Theoretician/Physician

Kama Suture when the surgeon
Has sex on his mind
Operating on you.

Karma when the stones
Jolt his memory/a necklace
His mother wore drowning.

Gall the taste below his tongue
Rendezvousing with his lover
Sipping wine the color of your medical experience
Spliced into a postmodern video:

The body as colony/invasion as cultural imperialism/
Your forehead logical pursuit
Of old stories layered within a new context.

He wears a necklace making love
What was your discomfort/stimulates
A body you never interfaced –
Washed and strung you are symbolism/tracking
On a single channel
Your medical condition/listed as drowning.

Global Shift

I spit gravel from between
My broken front teeth
And said,
"I never knew you kissed so bad."

Mother Nature shook my hand
Giving me a big grin.
"That was just a warm up."

The Regionalist

The half of you here is in dialogue
With the half of you there –
Her body flowering/humid.

The riverbed is rock/a peninsula divided.
A painterly regionalist planted in uncontrollable decay
Awakens the gods of old story –
Endings end with murder/polarize nudity/balance
Water reflecting stars
In songs requiring one voice.

Her dangling feet on a white train rapturously
Describe the smell of fragile immortality.

Her teeth on your neck are a bleached episode
Of moist
            mortality.

A snake enters paradise becoming the hole
It loves/to reach/your hand in and pull
Something out that belongs in there:
Folk songs and a shovel.

Her body is murmuring at the midpoint
Of a peninsula/in the present tense/shedding
Your skin.

Poetry is colored glass before time/her body
Speaks to you
            before glass/a chanting man
Thumbprinting
            the amber of her neck/undoing requires documentation

first the canary flies into the mine/second
footsteps echo to the amber of her pose:

Torchlight beneath her spine flickers like cinema –
A bracelet binds her upper arm splashing sunspotted blurs –
The spray of collarbone surf moistens her snail –

A chanting man eating the bonfire of her neck
(Below an apricot sun)
Restrains her hips
          helmeted by horn
Disembarking the vessel coated in ice
          flecked with defiant Naples yellow
Chanting sharpened stone
          stained raw sienna
Severing umbilical memory.

The twin eggs in his bag blink/petition/claim
Facial eyes
        are reproductive organs only.
               Only
Retina and pupils float in darkness –
Sinking through a tub of entrails –
Into his pitch black sac he wakes up screaming –

Her neck is liquid amber/his eye reproduces her
In his memory/pleasure
Dances dialectic hidden behind a veil:

History tastes like destiny dissolving/
Like quicksilver into loss/
            of memory/
She is biting his neck.

A boy shadowed awake his muscles burning
Two nights in a row/peas in a pod.

His father advances through curtains of slashing sleet.

Lightning the color of iceberg lettuce spread flat and jagged
Tears at the purple choking sky —
Charcoal funnels whirl and whine dust blinded
Driving straw through telephone poles —

His father is invisible —
The car big/full of shadows/touch and go
Past emptied jazz clubs and boarded up/nails
Sold by the
                pound/steakhouses.

Past a ferris wheel magnetically frozen
In a tight circle receiving
Butter colored jolts and bolts.

A pale nurse folds down a starched sheet.

The boy moves restlessly in his sleep:
Tidal waves of blue flannel crash/
Splashing the cowboy on his pyjamas.

His father shooting slaughterhouse rats
On the night shift dries his shoes on the porch.

A tangerine sun loosens its vermilion drawbridge
Above the small house; pillars;
Brick and vine of the grand institutions;
The art museum/hospital/meat packing plant/ivy
Covered University of Missouri.

8 lines × 6 syllables equals 48 units of sound
Since the turn of the century:

The boy's father listened
    beneath the campus trees
        Thomas Hart Benton speaks
            lounging with the students
        he's oil painting Harzfields
      the women's clothing store
    a hero tale made new
Transplanted middle west.

Missouri's favorite son (painter) finishes
With a (final) flourish
His allegorical mural depicting Hercules
                  defeating
The horned river god   Achelous
Personified as a   bull.

Dice are a by-product of horn
The boy's father-to-be gambled on his mother-to-be
She wanted to get-lucky-too.

Writing to herself/composing
The aroma of sandalwood/drifting
In a temple/transplanted middle west
A deity's numerous arms combed her like hair
Like a beautifully written letter/
She sailed home/floating/on scented words.

Late! Late! Her mother's discipline:
The catastrophe of perfection/an inquisition of symmetry
The torn fragrance of porcelain:

Snagged on a rose thorn/frozen by splattering/naked in the tub.
Ink inside the body never disappears.

Thomas Hart Benton creates the paintings
Lord, Heal This Child and *The Birth of Country Music*
Critics declare him a "regionalist":

Planting paper/burning the run-off/collateral
To the gods of syrup and hand-mashed brew;

Glues manufactured for sale across state lines
Invade the body leading to murder
And folk songs requiring one instrument.

Jackson Pollock ties a rope to a bucket in N.Y. City
Dripping paint like pissing

Cattle in their moment of terror –
The smell of skin dehaired by the burners –
Carcasses hauled from point A to B –
The boy's father firing at shadows –

Thomas Hart Benton flinging brushstrokes – up and across –
The taut bounce of canvas –

Children's twisted limbs prefigure newsreel footage –
Cadmium-yellow flames engulf crash diving Stukas and Zeroes –
Imagery he had no taste for his hand guided by allegiance –

Following the war/an explosion
Of abstract expressionism/elbowed him
To the edge of the art world.

He retreated to the heartland.

Ice Cream

Leaning into the window's opaque gliding woodwork
Bathed in a flashing red light
Eating ice cream to forget you
Neon flushes my heart valves:

The street below bubbles and pops like cooking oil
An Egyptian smears cobra crimson eyeshadow/

A truck driver bumps across railroad tracks into pink dawn
Aiming at a Celtic blade of mist revealed in a patch
Between buildings/

Silhouetted produce vendors drag boxes to the curb
Across a colonial nightmare bloodletting African sunset/

I flip my spoon out the window/

Streetcar doors fly open and clang shut orchestrating classical
European baby tongue slaughter in the grand concert halls/

Shoes echo their twin biting stone rose Peruvian teeth
Carved eons ago on a mountainside using simple tools/

Jackhammers hammer Chinese good luck carnation paper
Vibrating Spanish ankle sex twirling bullfighter capes/

Beneath a revolutionary flag somebody drops a coin
Into the newspaper box drive-by shooting poppy-stained/

Your strawberry whisper tells me the shirt I soiled
Smashing the bowl against the sink is too small/

The spoon falls slow motion ice cream on my tongue
Is sweet like a straitjacket/

I try to forget you because I never will.

Size as

It was bigger than Andy Warhol
Wider than an Aztec gold plate
Thinner than paper
Deeper than brain waves
Taller than the Statue of Liberty
Big enough to swallow us both
Acidic enough to disfigure our features
Herbal enough to boil us alive
Sad enough to keep us together
Orgasmic enough to chain us in bed
Raw enough to bury our faces
Tender enough to reflect a full moon
Busy enough to fill a suitcase
Tired enough to signal a destination
To sign a confession
To sigh for deliverance

It was deader than Andy Warhol
And as alive as conspiracy theories

It was all we ever wanted and could not have
It gave us life and almost killed us

It was impossibly possible and an endless
Story that couldn't get started

It ended on a high note
The black box was never found

I search my memory to greet you

You are as new as sepia in the hands of Giotto
Or one of his apprentices
With eyesight like mine.

Outside My Black Hole

Scales fell from the black pupil of my eye
Undressing you
    in a dangerous doorway a carbon
    undressing   copy of
The Mother Goddess
          pupil of my
   weep
Over the red shoe I punctured
               in a
my rattlesnake mouth/weep over the red/punctured
In a dangerous
         your armpits dark and kundalini
A carbon copy stretching for a higher
I punctured   bough/
      dressed in high heeled shoes.

The car too hot   led by you   crews
Hack at the Mother
        wreckage
           I opened one eye
Internalizing
        your feet   my
Rattlesnake   your feet this is
Your
    Mother/torn from their long march
        your carbon its black hole
I internalize
      your feet my pupil
Sucks in your tears   refusing
   carbon   to be Eve's eyes

stretching for a higher
I oversee blackened vegetation
        in a dangerous doorway.
The car too hot
                for your fingers tracing designs
On my skin
        dark and kundalini
        beyond
My skin gnashing   refusing
        designs of flight
                        on my skin
Our tattooed wedding bands disintegrate:
    a ring of Stalinist angels
                    /swords to the
Scales fell from
            /spine (glimmer) not really ethereally/weep over
Whispering
        "Go gentle into that good
Your red shoe   night." At the edge
The black pupil   of my black hole
        a gnashing of
                garden teeth
The Mother Goddess on skeletal fire
Grinning   my   head
Broken in the highway
Masturbatory   carnage undressing you/rib cage
            emergency crews
Pinned to the horn
                led by you at the edge
Of my black hole
                    weep
                I open one eye in a dangerous doorway.

Eurydice with High Heels

She gave herself comfort with an infantile ritual
Inviting me to brutally occupy her blanketed cave
And within another circle, her broken childishness.

Her skin called me deeper into her dark forest
My primal breathing broke the surface
Heaving solitaire/captured/conquering.

I was divining the landscape of our desire
Shattering the points on a compass
Mercury flooding a stairwell.

She sat in a tree growing roots of wet hair
I fed her her own brokenness
She asked for more.

I said, " … at the next moon,
When we descend again."

One Small Step

I handle your long black braid
Resting in a hollow of sinewy ocean,
Peeling your bark,
I *like* your skin raw.

My fingers are oily from the grief
In your private chamber;
Seeds receiving and transmitting, the old
Egyptian way, on top of each other,
To get a better view.

The moon looks so very different today.

Marry me telescopic. The curves of your body
Rolling circular, emergency fresh;
The mermaid and merman memory of longing
Between your teeth,
The moisture in your gaze
Compelling me into a darkness where
I take you *twice*.

Gypsy seeds impersonating Orpheus dance,
And prance, and pinwheel beneath the tough
Covering of my heart. Bleeding
Like a river of poppies in the underground
Poetry of resistance.

One small step on the moon/is so
Much smaller
Than anyone knew.

The Brother the Scientist and the Baby in the Second Voice

Eurydice is stuck in some oceanic hick town
Swallowing cold white lava
India ink skies invade the water in her blood
Starlight burns a hole in her tongue

Break the pepper shaker bones of a whale
Embedded within a skeletal context of desire
Wear a black turtleneck at midnight
Puff on a reefer play bongos
Intertwine yesteryear's sorrow with tomorrow
The color of your pupil foreground and vanishing point
Named by others name it yourself
Curving alone each circle a single curve unending
Paint your white cane the opaque translucence of
        modern dance
Bury straight lines in the Tower of Babel
Shake branches at the sun
Touch one leg to the green grass of home
Reach for a motionless tree
Weave and twist like the withered limbs of a crone
Balance your inner ear diving for pearls
Navigate a charcoal tunnel in the ceremony of ancient water
Extend your eyelid thin fingertips
Into the empty room of the world

Unbutton your lab coat swivel and sanitize Tutti Frutti
Impersonate Pat Boone
Sweet talk Eurydice bring her free samples
She says a person gets hungry other places too
Dance her to her knees smear her pink lipstick

Play her like she's got an I.Q. of 45 rpm
Unload your sewer of self-adoration:

She needs to cut a deal digging through history
Drenched in enchanted sunlight pitch black leaves
And stalks bend the wind would love to blow
The mythical day and night weathering her pale
Eyes pressed against the buffalo windows biting tall
Grass on her face the cool evening aims her only
Child at the ancestors snapping sticks beneath
The turtle leaping branch to branch into the sonnet
Of suicidal plunder –
Under dream time a walking stick clears land
For a new Hiroshima to live outside the law your fingers
Must be rich dark oozing in the beginning
The word was wet soil –

Fail to attain golden boyism
Split nutrients instead of the atom
Drink too many cocktails
Lift a record off her rhythm & blues hi-fi
Work your worm through the hole
King Cobra will nurse you

When she gagging rolls her eyes *Okay Einstein*
Whip the disc off your dick fling it
Against the mirror chipping Little Richard's tooth
Fold money into her mouth she counts half-ashamed
Looking into the pool of her infant's genetic curse
The town reservoir is cracking
One static channel on the black-and-white TV

Sit in momma's lap press your nose to the glass
Watch the world go bye-bye cross your eyes divide by four

Eurydice calculates miles to the gallon

She is inside starlight

You blink twice seeing once
A vision schism
An iris as beautiful as an iris
One eye whispering the other
Refusing to testify
Moving like a black dress through the wilderness

Her bare arms holding you are the driest branches
Your eye the sticky white flower of the world
Dissolving at the edges of a mist

An eye in the center of regret closes each morning
It has no twin

Around My Neck

I wake up with a good night's sleep hanging around my neck.

You didn't complain when I turned you over/tired
Of the moon.

Watching Orpheus with his harp you said wasn't a harp
Awake long enough to see Eurydice not make it out
Like a movie with subtitles not winning the Oscar
Knowing it needed the violence of Orpheus around my neck.

We search for each other in the dead places –
I want to bring you to me
And you want to know that.

Spit

Small poets with mangled thumbs
diatribing against the mythology
of tribes not their own.

Confusing facts with the spitting
of thumb tacks.

Pleasing those with a Howdy Doody head
but that'll never bring back
the lost love that prefers an authentic flavor.

Maybe she's got the good sense
to look before she sits down
and to taste what she's gonna sit on.

Some thumbs have pried open lids
where they never belong
and the stain on the page
typeset as if it knows all
is in the shape of a severed head.

They say after a guillotine falls
the head babbles
and egotism is just another form of execution.

Maybe that's why she left him.
He knew too much about nothing
and his #1 fan was the one
who childishly swept the floor.

Razor Sharp

Words pounded into trees the heart pouring an unlucky bottle
Wetting wooden typewriter songs of missing children.

Flowers spit teeth we drop watering cans
Dogs sniff out manifestoes smelling like trees.

Dig up lower case letters let your body be a bridge
To their laughter pounded into trees my heart is the hammer
Clawing echoes forever known as in the beginning
I used my body as a bridge to razor sharp stamens.

Let your body be a bridge to your fingertips kept
In your mouth overnight you know where the last memory
Is hidden half-filled.

Green sap bleeds into you through the lower case letters
You carried into the forest not because of any choice
You made.

Kill the dogs with your hipbone your body is a –
Don't suck your thumb their words pounded into trees
You tried to keep quiet I remember how empty
A bottle is a torso.

Wooden typewriters rise above the forest perfuming hereafter
In the beginning your body was a bridge dogs were raised on
The smell of your fingers what would happen if I found you?

My heart a manifesto bleeding into you razor sharp.

Switch On or Off

Elaborately prepare the reception area
Antennae weave jelly-like
Transparent in the sea of air,
                never forget who was declared
The prince of the power of the air
                      when you
Speak to yourself in circles or tongues circling
The wagons
        around a darkened dry reception area
Elaborately prepared
            with what is called love in some
       circles and time wasting
              by others.

At this point in the game those rooms should
Have been
        torn down years ago but you don't
Know what to replace them with
          because
          anything new may distance
The reception of what you don't
              want to say.

Punch-punch

The heat of your eyes in Turkey
The smell of your hair in China
The caress of your palm in Norway
The opening of your lips in France
The knotting of your brow in Paraguay
The unfolding of your leg in Peru
The arching of your back in America
The moon reflected on your nails –

The splintered palm trees reminding you
To forget about global warming –

Sexing my mouth on the rings around Saturn –
The pain in your chest pressed into my fingers –

I absorb you the way a hole punch
Sitting on top of an atlas invites
Negative space/
                    I assemble a Dadaist
Photo-montage:
Confetti swirls above a starving mother's belly in profile/

The moon is reflected on your nails/
I see a thousand year old garden through your eyelids/
Wishing:

I could reproduce you like antlers –
Like the smell of Baudelaire's flowers –
Before television flattened the roundness of our eyes
                                        your thighs
Beneath my salty tongue eating you with carnivorous pity
In my moment of greatest pleasure –

Ancient civilizations fly into curved glass
Smearing ice/smoke and moist foliage
Across your eyelids opening your eyes –
So dark and deep you are invisible/

I artfully assemble a photo-montage:

You howling with rage in the motherhood of language
Celebrating forgetfulness (with exactitude) on the rings
        around Saturn
Where I deposit antler music inside you:

Growing to disguise us in old age)   never)
Balancing us in crossing rivers)   never)

Curving with a certain degree of stretched out roundness
Anathema to European intellectualism)
                  perhaps)
                  smelling
Grass on your heels is all I've ever needed
You shrug your shoulders knowing
On the three occasions   – you most needed me
You found the exactitude   – of negative space
                     – holes on a map.

Idli Sambar

Music crawls up your leg
Enveloping you in eternity
As the clock strikes midnight
You search my kitchen
For rice flour whose odor
I associate with your fingers
Tracing my lips –
As music crawls up your leg.

Bell Jar Routine

You gong at me from the inside.
I caress your broken glass exterior
Covering you with my blood.

You talk into your pillow
Scratching my name.

Me thinking this bell has to do with
History

When really it's about percentages.

Rest of the Story Letter to My Love

Something sounds like a squeaky laundry pulley
Maybe raccoons this life we leave to our children
Its immensely depressed white blood my sweetheart
Listens Lake Superior sex horned tortilla blood cells
Percolating in salsa wearing purple bikini bottoms
Licking my history tells me my extension cord is
Long enough plug it in she's mascara streaked
Shooting star tongue going on about Daniel
Day-Lewis he's a doctor I'm partial to the girl
With the bowler on top of a mirror my love is thin
Thinks I want woolly mammoth memories T Rex
Sucking raw milk his eyes if you call them eyes
The madness of a tipped over honeycomb images
That carry power are the hardest to replace
Prisoners don't break out holes open where they
Are going if my handwriting was different I could
Love you better maybe I need calligraphy so
Nothing spills on you deer legs covered with
Bathsheba's oil walk me to the eucalyptus
Tree your hidden hair fresh as blueberries carnal
As a harem beaded and combed beneath shiny
Purple lips waterbed friendly waterbelly impaled
Grinding me this heat beyond air conditioning your
Eyes wanting me to defrost of course I'll
Plug it in —

The Knuckles of a Killer

Inside the tent at the front of the line
I look at a hand.

The fingernails are cut but the knuckles
are terrifying and that's what I've paid
to touch.

When the hand twitches I lean away.
Somebody outside yells, "What's taking all day?"

Killing stains the present tense
by erasing yesterday and tomorrow.
That's what's taking all day.

In the eerie glow of kerosene light
I look at my palm.
Why should I worry about my lifeline?
This is entertainment.

Did he kill his children? His wife?
Beat a man to death?

Maybe on a motorcycle
he was the right side of the law,
the cop tracking Bonnie and Clyde,
pumping machine gun bullets
into their bisexual tunnel of love.

The hand moves slightly in the deepening shadows.
How much of a cut does he get from this?

A voice outside yells, "Somebody die in there or what?"

I make my hand into a fist
upside down rub my knuckles against his
slowly bumping bone to bone
until it pulls behind black cloth hanging down.
"Time's up," says a bald guy holding a handkerchief.
"I used to be a coroner," he tells me.

We watch the hand reappear.

He spits on it.
The hand lunges like an alligator.

I'm in the shadows.
A little story runs through my head.
The hand is covered in blood.
It fires a gun.
It grips the bars of a jail cell.
It wants to wash a woman's face.

I step into the sunshine.

The knuckles on my right hand grow heavy.

Three

Thank you Little Miss Astonishing
For the bouquet you delivered
                along with three
Containers of yoghurt
                flavored
With the morning fog swirling around your vanishing point.

I could
                take one to work after I make
The bed smelling how you appear
                        convinced that before
Morning coffee I have betrayed you
                        three times.

I hear the cock crow
                and strangely enough sound waves
Pass out of me
                my red comb is your moon blood.
I think I'll eat the strawberry.

Over the Spot

Perfect love songs are annotated with
A toothpick thin sliver of ice shaved
From the sheet metal teepees
Stacked in your basement –
Painted with somebody else's images
Awash with sensuality and to a degree
Sentiment without overt sentimentality
Etched into your memory –
And suddenly in a dream between your teeth
Following a lonely meal
With friends who are your middle age uninsane
All of their thermometers neatly hung
And your question about metal freezing in unheated basements
Provokes polite chortling a raised eyebrow
One-upsmanship upside down in dark waters
Flashlights aimed at thermometers –
But the person who sent you the postcard
Is wearing a sweater because it's obvious
Teepees don't keep you warm unless someone else is
And you hesitate your gums bleeding
Certainly the people quoting Baudelaire
Don't want to hear pain is freeze dried
With a warning sticker from an accredited institution
Built over the spot where there once were teepees.

Re-divide

Fact is;
It was a mountain of quotations
(What we call the usual bestiary).

Climb to where you hear a certain distress calling you by name.
Maybe a situation you missed in real life.

Before you passed on
                into the chamber
                            of one particular sense,

A dimension you re-visit.
Before you see a hole carved just for you
Where you stick out your head
Seeing what you never could imagine.

Because *if* a soul could imagine this –
We'd use our senses the first time
And not spend a million years exploring every nook and cranny
                                        of memory

Before re-dividing
In the name of the father and mother.

A Warning

And suddenly I found myself involved
With the merchant class —
    what was to me
           a side of beef hanging
    in Rembrandt's window:
    a sound/the exchange of coin
Between sharp-eyed shopkeepers —
    a backdrop to Modigliani's fatal window
    asking
Why I paid too much.

My father had told me to wait
        and my mother pinched pennies
    her entire life
      she knew the value of salt
And we lived in a company town.

I rushed like a fool with open hands
Sketching myself as
        an underground cathedral/when really
        the hole in the bottom of the bucket
Was caused by heat
        hot enough to melt oil paintings.

Which would of course affect their value.

(D) × (D)

The voice of protest vs. derision of angels:
Division of angles/perspective
Outlawing flatlands/indenting
Irregular lower halves.

I left my heart in San Francisco/
Beep beep boop voice box.

A protest opening like starfruit
The purple pomegranate in the Ark of the Covenant —
From every angle the division of angels —

Foot pedal/slow motion/speeds up rainfall
Supercharged despair vs. the flat of the hand —
A surgical strike forced apology
The repentance of division/
The piss juice of the pomegranate/pray for me.

Stark relief in serpentine highway connections/
I left my heart in San Francisco
Beep beep boop voice box.

Slow shoes creak/topographical map rubbed raw/
The fat of the land:

Frank Sinatra can make it here —
Double breasted welcoming committee/pinstripes and
        prison stripes
The stinging lash on a hippie revolutionary
In Jerusalem/start singing the news/
Dirt roads paved under.

The division of transparent foliage/
Translucent flowers/
Opaque collisions/

The seed of Hiroshima vibrating a purple pomegranate —
The Ark of the Covenant dividing —
You're on guard duty. You explain.

Where were you? Beep beep boop voice box?
Romancing a stage hand?
Wooing that pretty young ticket taking tickets?

Your eyes search for the remote but this episode
Is on fast forward/so fast you've circled back
To the original concept:

A division of angels vs. the voice of protest.

How many roads must a man walk down
Covered in hair/staggering punchdrunk/
I've got a bellyache.
Where did I leave my heart? Don't worry —
The Inquisition keeps dinner jackets on hand/
Stop coughing/
It's not going to go away.

Momma told daddy to carve the flatlands/
Daddy told momma,
"We're gonna rock around the precipice tonight."

Equals

The cold water you drink
Equals the hot I pour –

The anger you feel
Matches my dispassion –

I flip a fishtail
You charge red flags –

I devour fresh fruit
And you daintily pick at a speck –

I am what you never told your parents
And you are what I never admitted –

You are the borders where I've never travelled
I'm the view of something new you crave –

I am a picnic with banjos
You are a temple of desire –

I am ravenous stamina
And you are a shell in my hand –

You provoke me with liquid silence
I respond with the roar of starlight –

You hear footsteps in the attic
And a door slamming downstairs
I roam the house with a baseball bat
Looking for impossibilities –

I hang the curtains for privacy
And realize I'm naked –
Is that why you laughed uproariously?

My memory is poor –
The essence of stuff lingers
Not the symbols/
I try to decipher the code word
And realize my personality is split –

You withdraw seashells I thought were cemented
I show you where the waters were born –

Valise

I travelled first class with the texture of your hair
In my valise alerting the conductor to the danger
Of my journey.

He held my hand as we passed through the mountains
Reassuring me I wasn't feeling your arms.

He told me the slice of bread I ate could have
Belonged to anybody.

He embraced me as I wept and said he saw no evidence
Of surgery to my heart.

He justified my actions saying he too would have
Pruned the overhanging branches.

He said the only connective psychic tissue
In any of this was my constant movement
For the past eight days.

He told me I would have trouble with the barbarians.
He said they idolized you.

Is This How Much?

We have never had so much of nothing.

A security guard
Not much more than skin and bone
Escorts me to the tower that was our love.

He gives me a gold coin to place on your tongue.

I owe you everything that I used to own.
But I don't own what you gave me.

Except for the look in your eyes
That once meant everything.

Is this how our ending begins?

You behind a wall growing thicker
Me on the other side
Collaborating with my negative emotions.
Call them the darkshirts.

Both of us paying taxes
To somebody called The Sun King
Whose embroidery you compliment
Walking arm in arm discussing horses.

And which one I will ride.

(D)

I am death between the strings of a violin/
In the wet sand clinging to your skin/

I am the palest moments of your desire,
A frayed rope,
And your pointing finger.

I am the home invasion staged by your parents,
And the black humor of a refrigerator light
Turned to stone.

I am the nakedness of teeth pressing into white flowers,
The shoreline you follow to Eurydice in your sleep,
The sadness beating at your eardrums like a forest fire.

I am your sister mortified on her eleventh birthday,
The evidence you swear to deny,
A book filled with black pages.

I am your mother giving birth to her accusers,
An evaporating tomorrow,
The statuette face down in the rain.

I am the thought you thought would go away/
I am waiting around the corner/

Aqua Sahara

You smile like a seahorse
Floating photographs into my mind
The color of water.

In a room with high ceilings
I fantasize dry land
Even though it burns beneath my skin.

You sleep with who I might be ...

In the birthing chair beneath my skin
The child of you is defined;
Where your arms meet the ceiling

And your toes climb the wall.

Impressionistic

I press myself into her skin
Moist, sticky and warm
Like a Caribbean wind,
Beneath our sheet
Of ice.

T

Because you lived many lives by the time you were nine

Because your language is like Japanese painting and the paper
Showing through

Because you disappear wearing white into the architecture
Of secrecy

Because your voice is a drop of water on a leaf

Because you breathe the inexpressible and sift it like flour

Because your lips work on me

Because your logic is rifle fire

Because I swim in the blood of your unknowing

Because you hold a pencil like it's your finger

Because you stand on a cliff and feel the wind
On my face

Coal

People say I look like him.
How he looked his first day back.

He couldn't stay away.
It was us on every channel in his brain.
The way our skin turned white when we slept
pushed up against the pink of our lips,
speckled with coal dust
smeared by his invisible fingers.

He couldn't stay away.
We were radio waves
defrosting the North Pole where his plane went down.

He made a final charge for the magnetic
fields
which bubbled in our mouths.

He typed late at night on a piece of black felt.
The temperature set higher than his furnace could take.

Star in a Manboat

In the house of stars
You wait in darkness for a white horse
Subverted by the geography of rational need
As well as the softness of a mid-morning shoulder
Explained as the body with a wing
Alone with its mate of negative space.

Day is a star misplaced
Arriving in the heart unannounced
Alerting stones
Who beseech their ancient cousins
To orbit cause and effect.

Travelling alone, light pursues historical revelation:
A chest becomes a boat.
You wait with a shovel.

Where emotions drown the surface beckons,
The horizon churns itself into cosmos,
Darkness refuses to masquerade as night.
What has no eye illuminates seeing.

Soil is not the final resting place for starlight
Blindingly pale in its love,
Immune to the bliss it sets in motion.
Burning like handmade paper,
Sighing like radar,
The chokingly sublime erupts
Or is suppressed magnificently.

Entombment swallows slavery
Ripening within a void,

Folding rays of light into something like rags: meaty;
The stone builds a house of thought.
Vibrations set invisibility alight –

Imprisoning dialogue must be translated/subtitled
And heavily exorcised – an alphabet
Dipped in gold upon the occasion of ground breaking day –
Noticed after the fact/quite impossible to explain.

You knelt on all fours beside an underwater fleet
Painted the apathy of unseeing/your spirit hovered
In the fog with only one breath until dawn.
You celebrated the first sunflower that became a threat.

A maiden tossing her white hair reached into you
Feeling the backwards running forward
Composing the composer.

Emotions dart across the expanse of textured sky
Within your shaded breastbone as if etched by Rouault.
Perhaps his background for a clown or the sky
To a crucifixion.

You grip the star like a lion's mane pulling you
Underwater past steel toothed gods demanding sacrifice
Within the concept of their creations.

You enter a temple.
The milk skinned maiden removes her gown.
Has the star brought you here? Have you brought it?

Does it desire another existence
Pushed endlessly uphill by a grieving postmortem archetype
Divinely undoing early stages of itself?

Star light, star bright,

Children's wishes designed by an adult eye or finger
Perform the penmanship of prophecy:
Nothing goes backward into wish sailing
With sails that catch the breeze /
The star does not create the chest.

Forward motion anticipates incarnation.
Legs kick inside legs trying to run with you.
A beginning going backwards to yourself.

Your history prepares you for this moment:
A lifetime of the plow working you.
Stars send a twin to wait like a fireplace
Counting what is white on your fingernails.

In social situations you smile politely.
Venom leaking out the corner of your eye,
Into the chest where feelings collide,
Like waves into surfers.

You are adrift in the temple of stars.
She twinkles with bracelets like a Gypsy
Training you in surgery / a theatrical event:
How crystal clear the cloudy skies that she fears heavy
Absorb moist heat /
Your root gives her sky.
She is soft as flesh and carved in stone.
You bend her into a receptive landscape
Providing the illusion of space / a wound.
She is muscular seen through a mist.
Her intelligence cuts like barbed wire.
You give her a dose of medicine to make her sleep.
Can the stars pass through you?
She wants more.

Her feet aim where she is going.
You look behind to see what she's walked out of.
Perhaps you look different now.
Your thumbnail is the same.
Stars shoot across the sky never sailing backwards
And once inside, neither will you.

Internal journey arrives/a circus pyramid of the dead:
Cause/effect/mercy.

Liquid stones blaze white heat
Mercifully memorizing the boundaries of your being.
Sunflowers impersonating arcs bow.

You open a book
To Edward Hopper's *The Nighthawks*.
Move out of the shadows
Entering the diner
The nighthawks go back to their coffee.
You look out the window/beyond the book/to that spot
Burned into your chest with liquid stone.
The nighthawks stroke each other like swaying coral
Swimming into each other where the food chain begins.

A series of misunderstandings
Leads you into an underwater cave.

There are as many mathematical rhythms
As shades of black in Rouault's palette.
Be your actions foolish or wise
You break the house of stars into a system:

Square – triangle – circle – square –
Circle – circle – rectangle –
Circle – triangle – circle – circle – circle – circle –

Triangle – half circle –
Circle –circle – circle – circle –

(pause)

(resume)

The horror-star of schoolboys taunting a turtle
With sparklers tied to sticks,
Thumping its shell with a club.
The eggs in the sand she crawled out of the river
To lay
Rolling down a hill.

Traces of archery shot long ago
By a hand tattooed differently from yours
Disappear.

The classical landscape reverts to an intellectual decision
Thought precedes rot.
At first you were young
Opening the lid to a firefly's prison
Concentric rings drew you into a mystery.

A flicker flew into you.
At the center of your birth was the world
Whose sun is a pale reflection
Of a much longer, more protracted death.
Mechanisms of intellect are the white horse
Hauling your boat-body containing a fist-fossil.

A sunflower traverses eternity to manifest within you
Not moving more than the length of your arm.
How you respond is decided by the mathematical rhythm
        you spawn.
Your roots are wet.

An elephant's ivory is his star/meat
Each night asking the core of the earth
How long must he memorize the universe.

The star you inherited etched
One small wing flying
With a bird of paradise tail.
You know the cost.
You showed it when you extended your hand
To write longhand,
Plotting a course within the following
Of an arc,
Scratched by circumstance like a glass eye
Plowed under.

Identity names a receiver of self.

A meteor enters your birth burning with crystalline ice:
Behind your eyes —
Within your ears —
And under your thumb.

With thanks to

Tanya Nanavati for inspiration and illumination

Luba Andrews for night-vision generosity and keyboarding
extraordinaire

Elizabeth Moore for eighteen trips around the sun

Bernard Kelly for deep-sea design, returning with fresh
anchors

Al Moritz for his literary telescope and light-touch
stethoscope

Allan Briesmaster, Colleen Flood and Pierre L'Abbé for
laser-like feedback

Felicia and Anne for games of wordplay and patience

Rosemary Banner for recollections of The Egyptian
Tea Room

David for reappearing

and

Robert Frost for writing *A Star in a Stoneboat.*